THE
PIZZA MONSTER

OLIVIA SHARP
AGENT for SECRETS

THE PIZZA MONSTER

by Marjorie and Mitchell Sharmat

Illustrated by
Denise Brunkus

Delacorte Press

To Each Other

Published by
Delacorte Press
Bantam Doubleday Dell Publishing Group, Inc.
666 Fifth Avenue
New York, New York 10103

Text copyright © 1989 by Marjorie Weinman Sharmat and
Mitchell Sharmat
Illustrations copyright © 1989 by Denise Brunkus

The trademark Delacorte Press® is registered in the
U.S. Patent and Trademark Office.

Library of Congress Cataloging in Publication Data

Sharmat, Marjorie Weinman.
  The pizza monster
  (Olivia Sharp, agent for secrets.)

  Summary: Wealthy secret agent Olivia Sharp helps
depressed Duncan find a friend.
  [1. Friendship—Fiction]   I. Sharmat, Mitchell.
II. Brunkus, Denise, ill.   III. Title.
PZ7.S529901   1989   [E]   88-30939
ISBN 0-385-29722-X
        Manufactured in the United States of America

                May 1989

        10 9 8 7 6 5 4 3 2 1
                HR

Who should you call when you're
in trouble?
Olivia Sharp. That's me.
My friends call me Olivia.
My enemies call me Liver.

I have a best friend, Taffy
Plimpton. But she moved away to
Carmel. The next day I went out and
got an owl named Hoot. She promised
me she wouldn't move away.

Hoot and I live in a penthouse at the
top of Pacific Heights with my
chauffeur, Willie, my housekeeper,
Mrs. Fridgeflake, and my folks.

But my folks
aren't home much.
This month
they're in Paris.

Mrs. Fridgeflake
is home all the time.
But as far as I'm
concerned, she might
as well be in Paris. She's always
busy flicking specks from glasses,
fluffing pillows,
and waxing plants.

Our penthouse has twelve bedrooms.
I use two of them. One to be myself in
and one to be a special agent in.

I have three telephones,
one of them red.

I wasn't always a special agent. After Taffy moved away, I used to sit around a lot in my furry white chair and look out my huge living room window at the boats going back and forth on San Francisco Bay.

Fantastic view.

But even when I looked at it with Hoot on my shoulder, I still felt lonely.

I'd never tell anybody that!

It was my secret.

My problem.

One night I said to Hoot, "I bet there must be a trillion secret problems out there. Waiting to be solved."

I'm good at solving problems, except for my own.

I'm good at keeping secrets, too.

I kept talking to Hoot. "If you're good at something, you shouldn't waste it, right?"

Hoot looked at me, silent but wise.

I could tell her answer was a definite YES.

And that's when I, Olivia Sharp, got into the agent business.

The next day I had Willie drive me to a print shop.

I had some ads printed up.

They all said:

Willie and I put up the ads around the city.

On telephone poles.
On street signs.

In store windows.
At the post office.

On school bulletin boards.

Everywhere!

Then I hooked up my special red telephone and I was ready for business.

I was setting up my files when I got my first call.

I answered immediately.

"Olivia Sharp, Agent for Secrets, here," I said.

I heard a sigh.

Then a voice said, "The world is coming to an end."

It was Duncan. I knew him from school.

"The world is coming to an end," he said again.

"That's what you always say." I strung three paper clips together. Why was he bothering me!

"I saw your ad at the pizza store," he said. "Can you help me?"

"I can't stop the world from coming to an end," I told him. "I'm good, but not that good."

"You don't understand," Duncan said. "I lost my best friend. Don't tell anybody."

"I'm good at keeping secrets," I said. "Stay put. I'll be right over."

I slammed down the receiver and rang for Willie to bring the limo around.

Then I went to the closet and got
my boa.

When I hit the street, Willie was
waiting with the limo. "Where to, Miss
Olivia?" he asked.

"To Duncan's, and hurry.
It's an emergency."

"You've got it, Boss," said Willie as
we rolled out of the courtyard and
through the big iron gates leading onto
Steiner Street.

While we rode up and down the hills to Duncan's flat, I remembered something. Duncan didn't *have* any friends. So how could he lose his best one? Duncan is *so* depressing. He's always saying that the world is coming to an end. And nobody likes to hear that. I know I don't, but a client is a client.

When we got to Duncan's, I told Willie to wait. I should have told him to give me a piggyback ride. Duncan lives in a flat on the fourth floor of a walk-up.

I was out of breath when I knocked on Duncan's door.

He answered it.

Duncan's hair was hanging over his eyes as if half his face was hiding from the world. His socks drooped over his sneakers, and his baggy blue jeans were slipping over his hips.

All of Duncan seemed to be on the way down. This guy was a real downer all right!

"**W**here did you lose this best friend of yours, and who is he?" I asked Duncan.

"It's Desiree, and I lost her inside Angelo's Pizza Parlor," he said.

"That's only around the corner," I said. "How could you lose her there?"

"We went into Angelo's to get pizza. I ordered a slice for her and a slice for me. When the slices came, I handed Desiree one of them. And that's when I lost her."

"You gave Desiree a slice of pizza and she disappeared? Did she go in a puff of garlic or something?"

I laughed and fluffed my boa.

Duncan never laughs. What with the world coming to an end and all that rot.

He said, "Desiree
didn't even eat her slice.
She got mad
and left the pizza
parlor. That's how
I lost my best
friend."

Duncan pulled
something out of
his pocket.
"I saved her slice.
Want it?"

Duncan dangled
a limp little piece
of cold pizza right
under my nose.

I stepped backward.
Then I looked
down at the pizza.

"This slice is very small," I said. "Was the one you kept for yourself bigger?"

Duncan shrugged. "I didn't measure them. I ate mine up and then I went home and called Desiree. But she hung up on me."

"Maybe you can get another friend. On second thought, that's not likely. I've got it. Get another pizza—a whole one—and give it to Desiree."

Duncan's face dropped. It was always doing that. "I'm out of money. I spent my last cent at Angelo's."

"Never fear, Olivia's here." I opened my purse and peeled off a ten-dollar bill. "This should cover it. Go back to Angelo's immediately and order a pizza to go. A large pizza with everything on it. Tie a huge red ribbon around the box. Take it to Desiree's house and give it to her. I'm glad I could help."

I went back downstairs to Willie
and the limo. It was a lot easier
walking down than climbing up.

I always feel I deserve a small reward
when I've helped someone. I had Willie
take us to the Bon Ton Chocolate Shop
for two of their superdooper ice-cream
sodas.

When I got home,
my red phone was ringing.

It was Duncan.

"How did it go?" I asked.
"Disasterville," he said. "Desiree said the ribbon was pretty. While she was untying it, I told her what was inside the box. Then suddenly she gave me a weird look and shoved the box back at me."

I had had the ice-cream soda too soon.

Duncan was still talking. "The box split open. The pizza slid out. Now I still have no best friend and I'm smeared from head to toe with tomato sauce, cheese, mushrooms, and anchovies. I look like a gooey pizza monster!"

I could almost see Duncan dripping pizza stuff. When I started in this agent business, I never expected to have a pizza monster for my first client. But I stayed cool. "I'll think of something else," I said. "You can depend upon Olivia Sharp."

"Hurry! The world is coming to an end," Duncan said, and he hung up.

I went to the window and looked out at the bay. A garbage barge was going by.

I knew what had gone wrong. How could I expect just one pizza, even with everything on it, to solve Duncan's problem?

I looked up Desiree's address.

I rang for Willie.

"Willie," I said, "find the name of a pizza bakery, and order fifty different kinds of pizzas to be sent to Desiree. Enclose a card saying *I hope you like one of these. From your best friend, Duncan.*"

"You've got it, Boss," Willie said.

That should take care of that, I thought. It's nice to be really, really rich and able to help others.

I stuck my feet up in the air.

I painted my toenails and wiggled them dry.

I fed Hoot.

Sometimes she hoots.
Sometimes she doesn't.
Sometimes I'm as wise as she is.
Sometimes I'm not.

I was in the bathtub when the red
telephone rang.

I grabbed my robe, rushed to my
office, answered my phone, and heard,
"The world has now come to an end."

It was Duncan, of course.

"Tell me about it," I said.

"Desiree just called me. She's madder
than ever. She said she doesn't want
fifty pizzas. What does she mean?"

"No problem," I said to him. "I'll look into it."

I hung up.

I had a real problem, but I never admit that to a client. Desiree had turned down a slice of pizza, a whole pizza, and now fifty pizzas. And she was very mad. There had to be more to this than a too-small slice of pizza!

I got dressed and rang for Willie to
bring the limo around.

"To Desiree's place," I said.

When we got to Desiree's apartment
house, we couldn't find a place to park,
so I told Willie to circle the block.

Five circles later, I was out of the car
and heading toward Desiree's front
door. She lives on the ground floor.

The fifty pizzas were blocking the way.
I picked my way through them.
I pounded on Desiree's door.

She opened it.

Desiree turned out to be one of those perfect scrub-a-dub-dub blondes who ties her hair back in a ponytail with a rainbow-colored ribbon. Without looking down I knew she'd be wearing shiny patent-leather, pointy-toed shoes that she could tippy-tap across the room in. I could see why Duncan liked her. Myself, I can't stand the type.

"I'm here about Duncan," I said, handing her my card.

Olivia Sharp
AGENT FOR SECRETS
I CAN FIX ANYTHING.
555-4848

I stuck my foot inside her door while I spoke. I wasn't going to take any chance she'd slam the door in my face when she heard why I was there. That's a trick we agents have.

"Come in," Desiree said without noticing that I was already partway in.

I flung my boa on the sofa in her
living room.

I said, "Duncan hired me to find his
lost best friend. You. Don't you know
it's wrong to get angry about a slice
of pizza?"

I knew that wasn't why Desiree was
mad at Duncan. I was fishing. Secret
agents have to do that.

"The pizza was just an excuse,"
Desiree said. "I don't want to be
Duncan's friend. He's so . . . so . . ."

"Depressing?" I offered. "Totally, totally depressing?"

"Right," Desiree said. "He's no fun at all."

"So why did you go into Angelo's Pizza Parlor with him?"

"He came along just as I was going inside. He said, 'Getting a piece of pizza? Me too.' So we went in together. When our slices came, he handed me one."

"And?"

"He said, 'Have a piece of this gucky, yucky, slimy pizza, which has dead cheese and dying mushrooms on it.' That's why I left. Do you blame me?"

Desiree didn't expect an answer. She folded my boa neatly and went on talking.

"Later on, Duncan brought a whole pizza to my house in a box tied with a pretty red ribbon. While I was untying the ribbon he said, 'Here's the slimiest pizza with all the guckiest, yuckiest things in the world on it. It probably died on the way over.'"

"That sounds like Duncan," I said.

"Yes," Desiree said. "He can even make Angelo's pizza look disgusting. Who needs a friend like that?"

Nobody, I thought. That was the whole trouble. Nobody.

I took a hard look at Desiree. She was tugging at her ribbon. Her rainbow was unraveling. Duncan can do that to you. Unravel rainbows and all of that.

But he was my client.
I knew what I had to do.
I grabbed my boa. "I must dash off,"
I said.
I left.
At the front door, the neighborhood
dogs and cats were
gathering around
the pizzas.

"Feast!" I called
as I got into
my limo.

"To the main library," I said to Willie.

The library has absolutely tons and tons of books. Willie whisked me there.

I checked out ten jokebooks.

"To Duncan's," I said to Willie.

When we got to Duncan's building, Willie helped me carry the ten books up to the fourth floor.

Duncan opened the door on the first knock.

We handed him the books.

"Here. Read these!" I gasped while I tried to catch my breath.

T hen Willie
and I took off.

When I got home,
my red telephone
was ringing.

I rushed to answer it.
But I was too late. No one was there.
I flung myself on the couch in my
office. This was an exhausting case.
The red telephone rang again.
Duncan was on the line.

"Where
have you been?"
he asked. "I've
been calling and
calling. Why did
you bring me these
dopey jokebooks?"

"To put a smile on your face."

"A smile?" he asked.

"Yes, a smile. That nice curvy thing under the nose that most kids have when they think cheery thoughts. Which, by the way, you never do."

"But you're supposed to help me with Desiree."

"Duncan, darling, Desiree's mad at you because you said awful things about the pizza. You say awful things all the time about *everything*. That's why Desiree doesn't want to be your friend."

"Are you sure?"

"Positive. Listen to me, Duncan. You just said the books I gave you are dopey. Have you even *read* them?"

"No."

"See what I mean? Now I've got something important for you to do, Duncan. Go to your window, look out, and tell me if you can see the world coming to an end."

"Hold on," Duncan said.

He put the receiver down.

I waited.

I tapped my fingers on my desk.
It was taking Duncan forever.
How big a job could it be?
At last he came back to the phone.
"I looked north and I looked south,"
he said, "but I didn't actually *see* the
world coming to an end. I couldn't see
east or west because there are buildings
in the way."
"Believe me," I said, "east and west
are in good shape. I checked on them.
Okay?"

"Okay," Duncan said. "So the world isn't coming to an end. But what do I do about Desiree?"

"Think happy. Read the jokebooks I gave you. Find a joke you really, really adore. Then call up Desiree and tell it to her fast before she can hang up on you. Then call me back."

I slammed down the receiver.

I waited for Duncan to call back.

I read my
horoscope.

I arranged my
credit cards in
alphabetical order.

I smoothed
Hoot's feathers.

The red telephone rang.

Duncan was on the line, laughing.
Laughing!

"I found five great jokes," he said.
"Desiree listened to all of them, and
she laughed."

"Super," I said.

"She says she's thinking about being
my friend."

"Now you're getting somewhere," I
said. "All you have to do is keep it up.
You don't need me anymore."

"You know Desiree was never my
best friend," Duncan said.

"I know it."

"*You* are!" he said.

"Not yet," I said.

I put down the receiver.
I made some notes for my files.

HELPED DUNCAN.

BE SURE TO FOLLOW UP.

RETURN LIBRARY BOOKS WITHIN 2 WEEKS.

MET A NEW GIRL, DESIREE.
SHE'S PERFECT, <u>NEEDS</u> <u>HELP</u> BADLY.

✷✷✷ MESSAGE TO MYSELF: ✷✷✷

SOMETIMES MONEY CAN SOLVE PROBLEMS.

BUT SOMETIMES IT CAN'T.

I closed my files and turned out the light in my office.

I went into my other bedroom to be myself.

Tomorrow I'm going to school.

Sometimes I'm a regular kid.

Sometimes I'm not.

About the Authors

MITCHELL SHARMAT and MARJORIE WEINMAN SHARMAT have written several children's books together and numerous books individually. The award-winning authors have now teamed up to create an original and amazing new series about Olivia Sharp, a helpful, problem-solving grade-school heroine who is in business for herself as an agent for secrets.

Marjorie Sharmat was born and grew up in Portland, Maine. She has been writing since age eight and is the author of nearly a hundred books. She is probably best known as the creator of the world-famous sleuth, Nate the Great. Mitchell Sharmat, a native of Brookline, Massachusetts, and a graduate of Harvard, is active in real estate and stock market investments when he's not writing books. His wildly popular *Gregory, the Terrible Eater,* a Reading Rainbow featured selection, has become a children's classic.

The Sharmats live in Tucson, Arizona. They have two grown sons, Craig and Andrew.